GW00762543

First published in the United Kingdom in 2000
by David Bennett Books Limited, United Kingdom.

Text and illustrations copyright © 1993 Graham Percy.
Style and design copyright © 1999 David Bennett Books Limited.

BRITISH LIBRARY
CATALOGUING-IN-PUBLICATION DATA
A catalogue record for this book is available
from the British Library.

ISBN 1 85602 320 6
Printed in Singapore

CHILDREN'S
FAVOURITE
ANIMAL
~ FABLES ~

RETOLD AND ILLUSTRATED
BY GRAHAM PERCY

CONTENTS

THE STORY OF THE FABLE

According to legend, Aesop was a slave living on the Greek island of Samos in the 6th century BC (before Christ).

People loved to listen to the stories that Aesop told. He was even invited to entertain the king's court.

The kind of story Aesop told was called a 'fable' – a short tale ending with a moral. His stories were usually about animal characters, and Aesop used them to teach people about the way they should behave.

Although Aesop never wrote down his stories, they were eventually recorded in Greek manuscripts in the 2nd century BC.

In the 1st century AD (*anno Domini* or after the birth of Christ), the fables were translated into Latin. In the 17th century, a French poet called Jean de la Fontaine rewrote the fables using this translation.

La Fontaine was born in 1621 in the Champagne region of France. He studied law in Paris but then turned to writing, and published about 250 fables between the years 1668 and 1693. His collections of fables were praised for their elegant style, and were translated into many other languages.

Eight of the most well-loved fables have been chosen for this collection. Each one has its own moral.

Slowly but surely wins the race

THE HARE AND THE TORTOISE tells the tale of a proud hare. When he challenges a slow, plodding tortoise to a race, he is sure that he will win. But the result is quite a surprise for both participants.

Always save for a rainy day

THE GRASSHOPPER AND THE ANT is the tale of a busy ant. She spends all summer preparing for the winter while her lazy neighbour, the grasshopper, does not think about the future.

Do not play mean tricks on others

THE FOX AND THE STORK is a warning to anyone who likes playing tricks on their friends. As the story explains, if you play tricks on others, you must expect them to do the same to you.

Brave ideas need brave action

THE CAT AND THE MICE tells the story of a family of mice who live in fear of a menacing cat. They have a plan to protect themselves, but none of them wants to put it into action.

A quiet and safe life is better than a luxurious but fearful one

THE TOWN MOUSE AND THE COUNTRY MOUSE warns us that luxury and splendour is not worth having if it also brings fear and misery. It is better to live simply but in safety.

Never trust people who flatter you

THE FOX AND THE CROW tells the tale of a cunning fox. The fox knows exactly how to get what he wants by complimenting and flattering a vain crow.

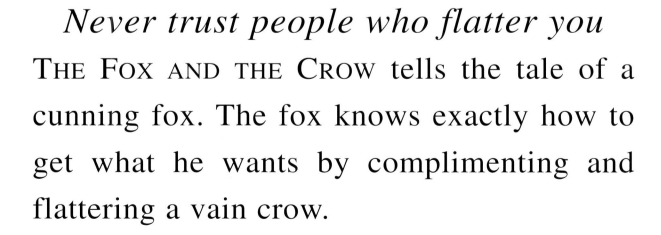

One good turn deserves another

THE LION AND THE MOUSE tells us how a strong, powerful lion chooses to spare the life of a little mouse. The mouse never forgets the lion's kindness and one day she is able to repay his good deed.

Do not be too choosy

THE HERON AND THE FISH tells the tale of a fussy heron who goes fishing for his supper. He decides that each fish he sees is not good enough for him and he ends up going hungry.

The Hare and the Tortoise

THERE ONCE WAS A PROUD HARE, WHO LIKED nothing better than showing off to anyone who would listen.

"I bet I'm the fastest creature in the whole world!" he boasted airily. "I can outrun *anyone*."

"And *you*," he sneered at a tortoise, who was standing nearby, quietly minding his own business, "you must be the slowest creature who ever lived."

The tortoise looked up thoughtfully and stroked his chin.

"Is that so?" he replied slowly. "Why don't we have a race to see if you are right?"

"*Me* …" giggled the hare, "have a race with *you*? Why that's ridiculous! That would be no race at all!"

And he rolled around in the grass, laughing at the very thought of it.

The tortoise ambled over to a tree stump.

"Let's start from here," he said. "We'll race all the way round the lake. The first one back to the stump will be the winner."

"No sweat," scoffed the hare. "I'll be back before you've even started."

The field mouse agreed to be referee, and the two animals lined up. The hare was still sniggering as the field mouse waved a twig and shouted, "ready … steady … go!"

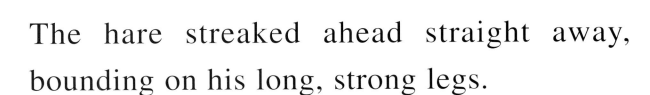

The hare streaked ahead straight away, bounding on his long, strong legs.

The tortoise plodded far behind him at his usual steady pace.

Halfway round the lake, the hare was a little out of breath. He stopped for a moment, and looked around for the tortoise. He was nowhere to be seen.

"I've plenty of time for a short rest," thought the hare, and he lay down in the warm grass. He was soon fast asleep.

A few hours later, the tortoise reached the hare. He smiled when he saw the hare fast asleep and snoring loudly. He didn't wake him, but just kept plodding along.

The hare slept all afternoon. By the time he woke up, the sun was setting.

"Oh dear me," he thought, "I must have overslept." He set off as fast as he could, but the tortoise, meanwhile, had almost reached the tree stump. The hare thundered behind him, closer and closer. But it was too late! The tortoise had won.

All the waiting animals crowded around the triumphant tortoise, laughing and cheering.

The hare sat in the grass all alone, and sulked for a very long time.

The field mouse referee was glad to congratulate the tortoise.

"Well done!" he squeaked. "Slowly but surely wins the race."

The Grasshopper and the Ant

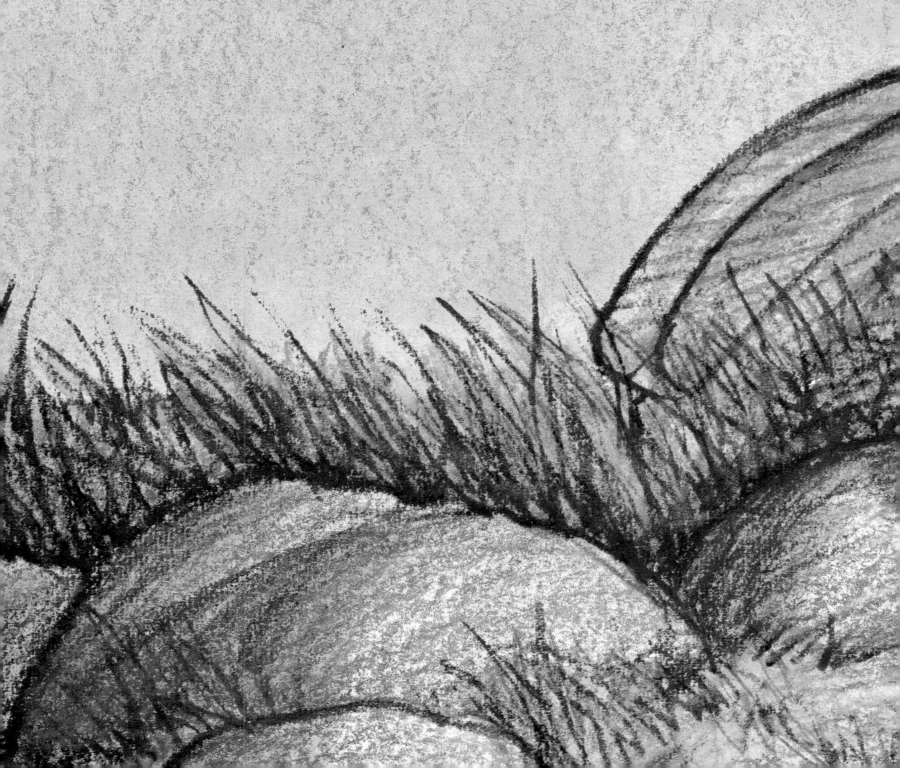

THERE ONCE WAS A BUSY ANT; A VERY BUSY ANT. Every morning she woke before sunrise, made breakfast for her little ones and then hurried out of the house, carrying an enormous sack over her shoulder.

All spring and summer, she scurried this way and that, collecting grains and seeds in her sack. She never went home before sunset, when her sack was full to bursting, and her feet and back were aching and sore.

The ant's neighbour, a grasshopper, was a cheerful fellow. But he was also very lazy. He loved nothing more than relaxing in the sunshine, singing and chirping all day long.

One hot summer's day, the grasshopper bumped into the ant. He thought that she was looking particularly tired and worn out.

"Why are you working so hard on such a lovely day?" he asked. "Won't you join me for a picnic?"

33

The ant put down her heavy sack and looked sternly at the grasshopper.

"I've no time for picnics," she said. "I've got to make sure my family has enough food for the cold months ahead. You should be doing the same."

The grasshopper just danced jauntily around her, saying, "but I want to make the most of the summer sunshine!"

The ant wearily shook her head, picked up her bundle and continued on her way.

35

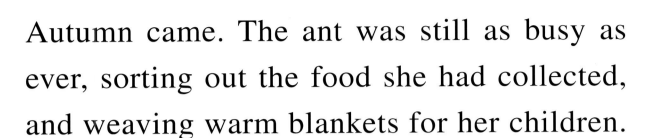

Autumn came. The ant was still as busy as ever, sorting out the food she had collected, and weaving warm blankets for her children.

The grasshopper just carried on singing and dancing. But the sunshine no longer felt as warm, and every now and then, when the wind began to blow, he would give a little shiver.

Soon it was winter. The trees were bare and snow lay on the ground.

The ant's home was warm and snug. A fire made of twigs crackled in the grate, and there were thick blankets on the beds. At every meal, the ant piled her children's plates high with food.

The grasshopper looked a sorry sight. He wasn't dancing or singing any longer. He was cold, miserable and very hungry.

In despair, the grasshopper went to the ant's house, knocked on her door, and begged for some food. The ant glared at him and said, "I worked all summer collecting food for my family, while you saw fit only to dance or sing. If you don't work in the summer, you can't expect any food in the winter."

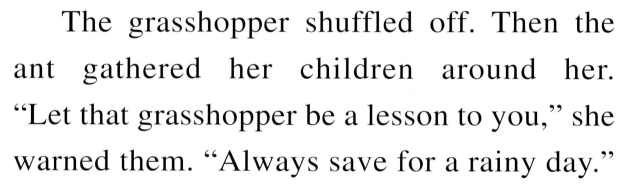

The grasshopper shuffled off. Then the ant gathered her children around her. "Let that grasshopper be a lesson to you," she warned them. "Always save for a rainy day."

The Fox and the Stork

THERE WAS ONCE A MEAN FOX, WHO LIKED playing tricks on his friends.

One day he thought of an especially good trick to play on Miss Stork. He sat at his kitchen table and carefully wrote her an invitation to dinner that night.

Miss Stork was very flattered by his invitation. She had never been to Mr Fox's house before.

"How kind of him," she thought, and went out to buy a new dress for the occasion.

The evening came. All dressed up, her feathers sleek and shiny, Miss Stork knocked at Mr Fox's door. "Come in, come in," smiled Mr Fox. "Dinner is ready."

Miss Stork eagerly sat down at the table, and Mr Fox brought in two dishes of steaming soup.

The smell was quite delicious, and Miss Stork's mouth began to water in anticipation.

Mr Fox hungrily lapped up his steaming soup. But, try as she might, Miss Stork couldn't drink a single drop. Her narrow beak was far too long for the shallow bowl!

Mr Fox looked up from his empty bowl. "I'm *so* sorry you don't appreciate my fine cooking," he said, with a sly, greedy grin. "Let me help you." And in no time at all, he had gulped down Miss Stork's soup as well.

Miss Stork was absolutely furious at Mr Fox's trick, but she didn't let her anger show.

"Mr Fox," she said, smiling sweetly, "you have been *so* kind. Do please join me for dinner at my house at the same time next week." Then Miss Stork flew home, very hungry indeed.

The following week, Mr Fox arrived promptly at Miss Stork's house. He was wearing his best suit and his shiniest shoes, and carried a large bunch of stolen red roses.

"Do come in," said Miss Stork, smiling. "I'm just putting the finishing touches to dinner in the kitchen. Won't you join me?"

Mr Fox watched keenly as Miss Stork stirred her soup. He licked his lips. He was absolutely ravenous.

Then Miss Stork poured the soup into two tall jars with long, thin necks. Dipping her slender beak into one jar, she quickly drank up her soup.

But the hungry fox couldn't reach a single drop. His snout was far too short and stubby.

"I'm *so* sorry you don't appreciate my fine cooking," mimicked Miss Stork. "Please let me help you."

The famished fox watched in dismay as Miss Stork drank up all his soup as well.

As Mr Fox said goodbye to Miss Stork, she smiled her sweetest smile.

"Thank you so much for coming," she said, "but do remember – if you must insist on playing mean tricks on other people, they may well play tricks on you too. Goodnight."

The Cat and the Mice

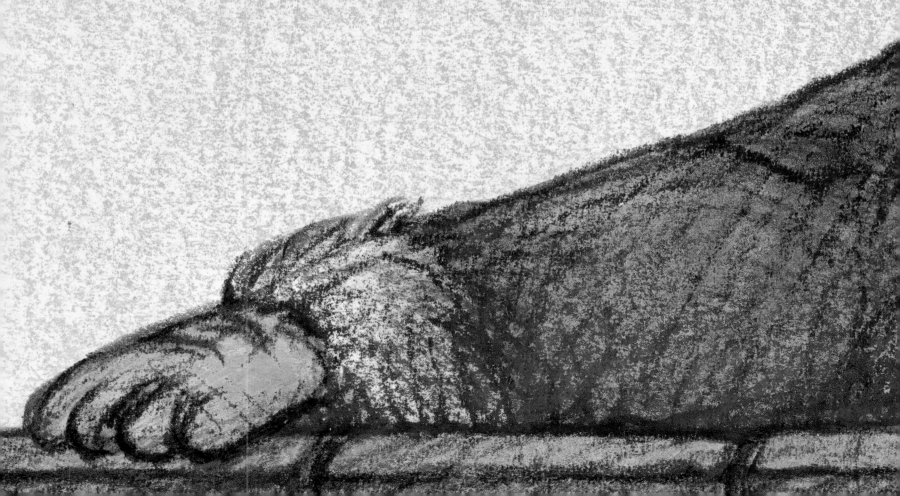

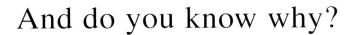

THERE WAS ONCE A LARGE FAMILY OF MICE, who lived together in a little house in the country. Life for them should have been peaceful and happy, but it wasn't.

And do you know why?

A large, prowling ginger cat made every day a perfect misery for the mice. Each morning, the cat crouched outside the back door, watching the family eat breakfast. The little ones trembled in fear as the cat's shadow fell across the breakfast table.

After breakfast, the older mice dashed to the hedgerow to gather food. They scuttled busily about in the tangled undergrowth, freezing in terror whenever they spied the cat's swishing tail.

In the afternoons, Mother mouse liked to tend her little garden. But whenever the tips of two furry ears suddenly appeared over the bushes, Mother mouse would run indoors, her weeding left unfinished.

After tea, the two mouse twins would start their music practice, but the sound of their playing would soon be drowned out by a dreadful mewing from outside.

In the evenings, when Father mouse was closing the sitting room curtains, a great, shiny eye would appear at the window, watching his every move. Father mouse would shrink back against the wall, terrified to bits.

One day, Grandma mouse and Grandpa mouse came to stay. They were sitting quietly on the terrace when, suddenly, a huge paw appeared from nowhere. Grandma and Grandpa had to run for their lives.

"This is absolutely ridiculous," gasped Grandpa mouse. "Surely there must be something that you can do to protect yourselves from that menace."

"I agree," said Father mouse and he called an emergency family meeting in the kitchen. Straight away, Mother mouse had an idea.

"If the cat had a bell tied around her neck," she suggested, "we'd always know exactly where she was, and have plenty of time to get away from her."

"What a wonderful idea!" said Father mouse, giving his wife an admiring hug.

Grandma mouse, who hadn't said anything so far, shook her head and tutted loudly. "And which one of us is *actually* going to put the bell around the cat's neck?" she asked, tartly.

"We can't," said the little mice, looking nervously at each other. "We're too small."

"We can't," said the bigger mice in trembling voices. "We're too scared."

"We can't," said Mother mouse and Father mouse. "We're too slow."

"We can't," said Grandma mouse and Grandpa mouse. "We're too old."

Father mouse sighed with exasperation.

"It may be easy to think of difficult things to do," he observed, "but it's not so easy to put them into practice!"

The Town Mouse and the Country Mouse

THERE WAS ONCE A LITTLE BROWN MOUSE, who lived happily among country hedgerows. Each day, he roamed the woods and fields, looking for tasty berries, fruits and nuts to eat. Each night, he snuggled into his warm, comfortable bed in his little home under an old oak tree.

One day, this country mouse invited his cousin, a town mouse, to stay. He gave him a delicious supper of berries, nuts and apples, and even gave up his own mossy bed for his cousin each night.

But the town mouse was not impressed.

"I don't know how you can stand living here," he said, rudely. "It's such a bore having to go out to find every meal. Besides, your bed is lumpy. Come home with me and I'll show you what life is *really* like."

What an adventure! The country mouse was thrilled. He packed his bags and they set off together.

The little country mouse had never seen anywhere as large and as grand as his cousin's house.

Once inside, the town mouse led his cousin into the grand dining room. The country mouse was open-mouthed at the feast laid out on the table. There were bowls of nuts, platters of cheese and plates of cakes and biscuits.

"Help yourself," gestured the town mouse, elegantly reclining on a cake stand. "This is how we town mice eat every night of the year."

The country mouse squeaked with delight and started to nibble an enormous hunk of cheese.

He had scarcely taken two bites, when he heard a fearsome mewing. A large cat entered the room. The two mice, quite terrified, immediately rushed to hide behind a large bowl of fruit.

Luckily for them, the cat merely prowled around the table, then left. The mice breathed a sigh of relief and crept out from their hiding place.

However, just as they were about to start eating again, they heard a frightful barking, and a dog bounded into the dining room.

"Oh no," wailed the country mouse.

The mice leapt off the table to hide behind a clock on the mantelpiece. The dog sniffed about for what seemed like hours. Then he heard his master calling him, and padded out of the room.

The country mouse had never been so scared in all his life. He shook his head and wiped his brow.

"If *this* is the way you live every night of the year," he said, "then this isn't the life for me. I'm going straight back to the country."

The town mouse sadly reached into his waistcoat pocket and drew out a tiny pencil and a scrap of card.

"Write something for me to remember you by," he said, and handed the pencil and card to the country mouse.

The country mouse took the pencil and carefully wrote a message, then gave the card back to the town mouse.

This is what it said: 'A quiet and safe life is better than a luxurious but fearful one.'

The Fox and the Crow

ONCE THERE WAS A BIG, BLACK CROW, AS proud and as vain as could be. He strutted around the countryside, showing off to all the animals.

"What a very fine fellow I am!" he would say when he saw his shadow on the ground, or caught sight of his reflection in a pond.

One day, he passed a small farm cottage with an open door. Being nosy as well as conceited, the crow hopped through the door and found himself inside a little kitchen.

The farmer and his wife had left the remains of their lunch on the table. There was bread, butter, milk and … cheese.

"Aha!" said the crow, with a gleam in his eye. "Cheese! My favourite."

He flapped onto the table, picked up the largest chunk of cheese, and carried it away in his beak to a nearby oak tree.

Little did he know that a fox had been watching him from behind a row of cabbages in the cottage garden.

The fox was very hungry, and wanted the cheese for himself.

"I know that crow won't share it with me," he thought, "and I can't climb the tree and grab it from him. How on earth can I get hold of it?"

He thought and thought, and then he had an idea. He strode over to the base of the tree and, cupping his paws around his mouth, called up to the crow.

"Good afternoon, Mr Crow! I'm so glad to make the acquaintance of such a fine fellow as you. How stunning you are with your mighty wings, your gleaming feathers and your graceful neck. I've heard you can sing *so* sweetly. Would you be so very kind to do me the honour of a song?"

The crow was so flattered, he could not contain himself.

He stretched his neck, ruffled his feathers and shuffled along the branch to get into a good position to sing for the fox.

The crow opened his mouth to sing … and out fell the cheese!

Down below, the fox was waiting with his big mouth open wide. The cheese fell straight in, and the fox happily gobbled it all up.

The crow watched in dismay as the last crumbs of the delicious piece of cheese disappeared down the fox's throat.

Two sparrows had been watching everything from the garden gate. One of them cheeped wisely to the other, "I can see that you should never, ever, trust people who flatter you."

The Lion and the Mouse

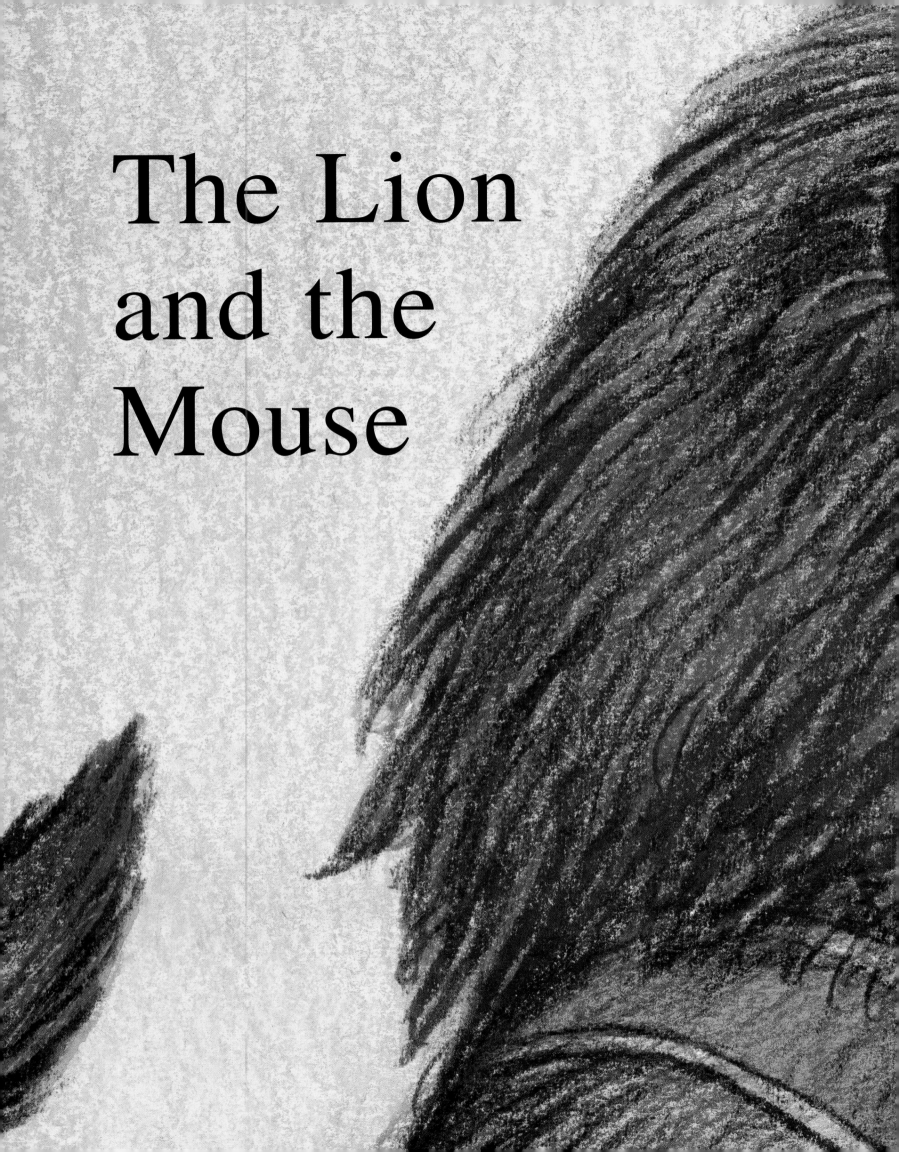

ONE DAY, A TINY MOUSE WAS RUSHING THROUGH the forest. She had been searching all day for food, and was carrying an ear of wheat home for her children.

The mouse was very anxious to go back, for her children were all alone, and she was also very tired. Just then, she came to a brown tree stump. It looked so soft and inviting.

"Just five minutes won't hurt," she thought with a yawn, and settled down for a quick, refreshing nap.

As soon as she shut her eyes, she heard a terrible roar above her. The tree stump shifted and shook, and the mouse found herself trapped in a lion's paw. She had not been sleeping on a tree stump at all, but on a lion!

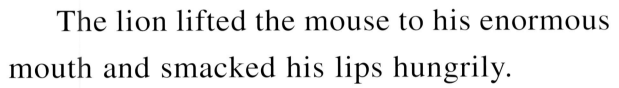

The lion lifted the mouse to his enormous mouth and smacked his lips hungrily.

The little mouse cried out in great anguish, "oh king of beasts, please, please spare me! I'd be *such* a meagre meal for you – a mere mouthful. My poor children are waiting for me. Please spare me!"

The lion paused.

"And you never know," the mouse added hastily, "I might be able to help you one day."

To her surprise, the lion burst into peals of laughter. "How could a tiny mite like *you* help an enormous creature like *me*?"

Gently putting the mouse down, he laughed, "I can't see how you will *ever* be able to help me, but since you have made me laugh, you may go free."

He was still laughing as the little mouse disappeared through the ferns into the forest.

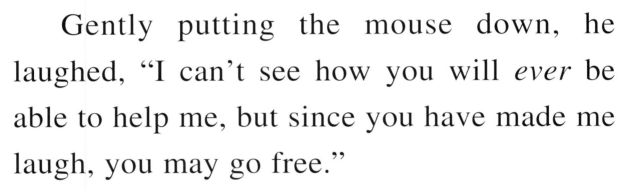

Some days later, the lion was roaming through the forest looking for food, when all of a sudden …

WHOOSH!

He tripped over a rope, and a hunter's net fell down on top of him. The lion twisted and struggled. He pulled and kicked. He scratched and tore. But no matter what he did, he could not get free. He was trapped.

The lion raised his head as far as he could, and roared with anger.

Far away, on the edge of the forest, the little mouse heard the lion's angry roars.

Straight away, she rushed to find him. Clambering over mossy rocks and scurrying along fallen branches, she ran as fast as she could, until she reached the clearing where the lion lay.

Without stopping to think, she scampered up onto the lion's back, and began to gnaw at the thick ropes that held him fast.

She gnawed all night and half the next day until, at last, the net fell apart. The lion crawled out. He stretched his legs and shook his mane with relief. He was free!

"Thank you, little one," said the lion, gratefully. "You have saved my life. But why did you bother to help me?"

The little mouse replied solemnly, "even between the grandest and tiniest of creatures – one good turn deserves another!"

The Heron and the Fish

ONE FINE AFTERNOON, A PROUD AND ELEGANT heron was strolling along the bed of a sparkling stream. He had spent the morning admiring his reflection in a pool, thinking what a very fine creature he was. Now he was beginning to feel peckish. What could such a fine fellow as he have for supper?

Just ahead of him, at a bend in the stream, two fat perch were playing. They were so wrapped up in their game that they didn't notice the heron approaching.

The heron could easily have gobbled both of them up then and there, but instead he strolled on past, his beak in the air.

"Far too common and tasteless for me," observed the heron. "I can't be bothered even to open my beak for them."

Further along the stream, under a willow tree, the heron saw two large trout tumbling about together. The water churned and foamed as the fish chased each other around and around in circles.

The heron shook his head as he passed them.

"Far too much trouble to catch," he complained. "I'm sure to find something much better around the next bend."

He strolled on.

A shoal of tiny minnows darted between his feet. The heron looked at them in disgust.

"Far too small and bony," he sneered. "A heron of my size needs much bigger fry than those meagre specimens."

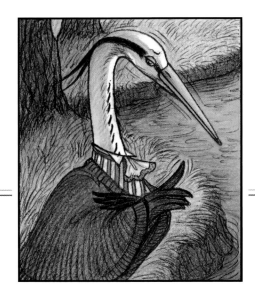

119

The heron strutted on, peering down into the water. It wasn't long before he saw a fat carp resting in the shadow of the bank.

"Far too scaly for me," muttered the heron, and he strolled on, grumbling under his breath, "will I find nothing to eat today?"

By now, the heron was beginning to feel very, very hungry indeed. The sun was starting to set, and he realised that it would soon be dark. Before long, he wouldn't be able to see anything at all in the water.

In desperation, the heron swished his beak this way and that among the pebbles and weeds, looking for something – anything – to eat for his supper.

At last, he found a tiny snail. With a frantic swoosh of his beak, he scooped it up and gulped it down his throat.

All the fish gathered in the gloom to watch the heron. They pointed their fins at him, and giggled and gurgled at his pathetic supper.

A wise old toad, who had been watching the heron all day, stroked his chin and said loudly, "folk who are too choosy often miss out altogether."